W9-CLW-628

When I'm Feeling
JeALOUS

Written and illustrated by Trace Moroney

The Five Mile Press

When I'm feeling jealous
I feel like a big, green, grouchy monster.
I see the things others have
and want to have them all to myself.

When I'm feeling jealous
I feel like Mum and Dad
love my little brother more
than they love me.

Feeling jealous can sometimes
make me do silly things to try and get
someone to notice me.

Some things just make me
so jealous . . . like when
someone has a new toy
that I want . . .

or when someone beats me in a running race
(and comes first!) . . .

or when someone is getting more attention than I am.

Feeling jealous makes me think about
all the things that I don't have –
and the things that I am not very good at.

This doesn't make me feel very good
so . . .

When I'm feeling jealous
I try to remember to appreciate
the things I do have –
and the things that I am good at . . .

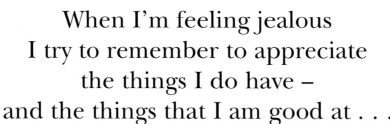

like my favourite toys . . .

and being good at skating . . .

and knowing that I am a really
kind and caring friend.

Talking about why I'm feeling jealous
makes me realise that my friends and family
love *me* for just being *me*!

Jealousy is when it seems like
others have a lot more
(or can do a lot more) than I can.
Sometimes they do,
sometimes they don't . . .
and sometimes
those same people
may be jealous
of *me*!

Background Notes for Parents

Self-esteem is the key

The greatest gift you can give your child is healthy self-esteem. Children who *feel valuable*, and who *trust themselves* have positive self-esteem. You can help your child *feel valuable* by spending quality time with him or her, playing games, reading books, or just listening. You can also help children *feel valuable* by helping them discover and become the person they want to be. Success follows people who genuinely *like who they are.*

However, happiness is more than just being successful. Helping your child gain the *self-trust* needed to deal with failure, loss, shame, difficulty and defeat is as important – if not more so – than succeeding or being best. When children trust themselves to handle painful feelings – fear, anger and sadness – they gain an *inner* security that allows them to embrace the world in which they live.

Each of these *FEELINGS* books has been carefully designed to help children better understand their feelings, and in doing so, gain greater autonomy (freedom) over their lives. Talking about feelings teaches children that it is normal to feel sad, or angry, or scared at times. With greater tolerance of painful feelings, children become free to enjoy their world, to feel secure in their abilities, and to be happy.

Feeling JEALOUS

A healthy self-esteem will help your child deal with painful feelings of jealousy when they arise. It's natural for a child to feel jealous sometimes. Jealousy expresses a deep fear of unimportance compared with others. Children can become jealous of another child's toys, abilities or even friendships. You can help your child cope with jealous feelings by teaching them how to love and value who they are, regardless of what toys, abilities or friendships they have. When your child values themselves from the inside it matters less how they compare with others. Playing together, talking together and doing things together will help your child feel valued, trusted and important with little reason to feel jealous.

Written by psychologists Bill Hallam and Dr Craig 01sson

To those who continually seek more...when,
within ourselves we have enough.

The Five Mile Press Pty Ltd

950 Stud Road Rowville
Victoria 3178 Australia
Email: publishing@fivemile.com.au
Website: www.fivemile.com.au

First published 2007

Illustrations and text copyright © Trace Moroney, 2007
All rights reserved

National Library of Australia Cataloguing-in-Publication data
Moroney, Trace, 1965
When I'm feeling jealous.

For children
ISBN 978 1 74178 358 2 (hardback)
ISBN 978 1 74178 359 9 (paperback)

1. Jealousy - Juvenile fiction. I. Title.

A823.3

Printed in China 5 4 3 2

Prints of artwork produced for this title are available for purchase.
Please email Trace Moroney on tracemoroney@xtra.co.nz for more information.